Anna's Book

BY
Barbara Baker

PICTURES BY
Catharine O'Neill

DUTTON CHILDREN'S BOOKS · New York

For Babbie
B.A.B.

For Anne Miller
C.O.

Text copyright © 2004 by Barbara A. Baker
Illustrations copyright © 2004 by Catharine O'Neill
All rights reserved.

CIP Data is available.

Published in the United States 2004 by Dutton Children's Books,
a division of Penguin Young Readers Group
345 Hudson Street, New York, New York 10014
www.penguin.com

Designed by Irene Vandervoort

Manufactured in China   First Edition

1 3 5 7 9 10 8 6 4 2

ISBN 0-525-47231-2

Here comes Anna.

Anna has a new book.
Anna loves that book.

Mommy sits with Anna.
Mommy reads
the whole book.

"The end," says Mommy.

"Again," says Anna.

Mommy reads the book again.

"The end," says Mommy.

"Again," says Anna.
"One more time," says Mommy.

Mommy reads *the* book again.

"The end."
Mommy is finished reading.

Anna gets Teddy Bear.

Anna reads her new book to Teddy Bear

"Again," says Teddy Bear.

Anna reads her new book
again and again
and again.

Anna and Teddy Bear love that book.

The End.